DAVID FLUSFEDER has written seven previous novels, including *John the Pupil* and *The Gift*. His most recent book was the non-fiction *Luck*. He was born in New Jersey but has lived mostly in London. He is currently on the East Kent coast.

ALSO BY DAVID FLUSFEDER

Luck

Army of Lovers (with Mark Springer)

John the Pupil

A Film by Spencer Ludwig

The Pagan House

The Gift

Morocco

Like Plastic

Man Kills Woman

Something Might Fall

DAVID FLUSFEDER

CROMER

PUBLISHED BY SALT PUBLISHING 2026

2 4 6 8 10 9 7 5 3 1

Copyright © David Flusfeder 2026

David Flusfeder has asserted his right under the Copyright, Designs and Patents Act 1988 to be identified as the author of this work.

This book is sold subject to the condition that it shall not, by way of trade or otherwise, be lent, resold, hired out, or otherwise circulated without the publisher's prior consent in any form of binding or cover other than that in which it is published and without a similar condition including this condition being imposed on the subsequent publisher.

This book is a work of fiction. Any references to historical events, real people or real places are used fictitiously. Other names, characters, places and events are products of the author's imagination, and any resemblance to actual events or places or persons, living or dead, is entirely coincidental.

First published in Great Britain in 2026 by
Salt Publishing Ltd
12 Norwich Road, Cromer NR27 0AX United Kingdom

GPSR representative
Matt Parsons matt.parsons@upi2mbooks.hr
UPI-2M PLUS d.o.o., Medulićeva 20, 1,0000 Zagreb, Croatia

www.saltpublishing.com

Salt Publishing Limited Reg. No. 5293401

A CIP catalogue record for this book is available from the British Library

ISBN 978 1 78463 371 4 (Paperback edition)
ISBN 978 1 78463 372 1 (Electronic edition)

Typeset in Neacademia by Salt Publishing

Printed and bound in Great Britain by Clays Ltd, Elcograf S.p.A

1

1970

THIS FALLING WOMAN who sees it all, exalted, her husband a Park Avenue doctor, her son gentlemanly and still in grade school, her books, at least one of them, best sellers. It had been adapted for the movies and this has attracted notoriety as well as fame, her husband's back stiffens when they are led to the best table in the best restaurants, his hand a little too forceful against the small of her back, as eyes flicker to them and away and back again, *That's her, and him* . . . The adaptation that had been in all the movie theatres starred an up-and-coming actress who was about to marry a rock star, and was, everyone said, a shoo-in for the Oscar. The actress had dyed her hair black for the role to look more like Emma Hoffman, and *obviously* it was based on her life, it had to be, the unfulfilled, unsatisfied hostess wife, the fussy doctor husband with his mother's boy needs and laughable sexual technique and his affairs, the emptiness at the heart of Upper West Side late-1960s life, the sidewalks and windows and rooftops so fraught with dangers, because at any moment something might fall, perhaps herself . . . And of course it is exaggerated for fictional purposes, *of course* it is, and of course it had all been further exaggerated for the movies, we all know how that works, we're not children . . . but nothing is written in a vacuum, energy cannot be manufactured or destroyed, only transformed, and she had always been an autobiographical writer, turning the stuff and discontents and, on occasion, the magic, of her own life into books, that assimilated Long Island childhood, the abortions at Vassar, the dreams of leaving, the dreams of having it all.

There is no shame in desire, at least there shouldn't be, and everyone agrees on how *brave* she is, in her fiction if not in life, how willing she is to own up to unhappiness, the brightness of the light she shines on to the elements of her life and of her self; and if her husband's smile is unnaturally pleasant, her own eyes a little too sparkling—and how she longs to put those Gucci sunglasses back over her damaged hurting eyes, but she may not, because then she would attract even more attention, *Who does she think she is . . . ?* which is such a good question because she doesn't know who she is, and she'll have the salad, with the dressing on the side, and maybe just a fillet of fish, broiled, no sauce, and her husband, with his clerkish attention to the leather-bound wine list, his filet mignon and baked potato with sour cream and chives, and yes, why not, the *minestrone* to start, and she tries not to wince at his attempt at the inflections of an Italian accent, and he pretends not to notice that she has winced, just as he pretends not to notice the glittery bright darkness that surrounds them, that they carry with them everywhere they go, to this restaurant, to that art opening, to their seasonal 'at homes'. He has stopped going with her to the perpetual double bills at the Thalia, he had made it more difficult for her to fill her prescriptions for Valium and Seconal, and he has come almost to prefer the rages when she comes back from the drugstore *humiliated*, to that silence, the heartache, the sadness that he has done nothing to alleviate, in whose cause he is maybe implicated.

She blames him, even if she protests that she does not, she apologises, she makes that brittle little laugh that had so charmed him with its sophistication when they first met at the yacht club in Port Washington and which is beginning to appal him now, she could remind him of that night of confession they made the week before the wedding, sitting in the car on the way to Montauk Point to visit her family, and he had thought this was about the rumours of her being *easy*, and it was about putting to rest the ghosts of old lovers, his, appeasing her jealousy, because back then she might spark into jealousy, she was so proprietorial, he felt sometimes like she was a lioness and he was her cub, or maybe her *prey* . . . and they sat in the car and she ignored him when he said that maybe they should resume their journey, because what time were they expected? and wouldn't it be kind of rude not to be there yet, maybe they should find a payphone and at least let them know . . . ? But, instead, *Who was after that?* or *Who was before that?* or *What was her name?* and *Did you make her come?* which shocked him, not because she was thinking like that, or talking like that, that was part of her appeal for him, part of who she was, so much more daring than anyone he knew, so much more daring than he, but he recognised in these moments that he carried his parents somewhere inside him, and he prickled as they would prickle, which caused him a double kind of shame. And after it was all told, he even added a couple, girls he had kissed but never screwed, to give himself some shinier patina, to make himself more worthy of her, *I won't let you down, I won't . . .* and then it was her turn, and yes, there were more boys than he had had girls, even with the ones he had falsely added, and the ones she has falsely subtracted, but that wasn't what this conversation was about, not for her, she said their names in a flat mechanical voice, like an insomniac trying to bore herself back to sleep, that was just the prelude to something else, the real substance of the conversation, which was the warning that she wanted to give him, he could get out now, get away now, she would find some story to tell that wouldn't reflect poorly on him, but you should know what you're letting yourself in for, let yourself know who you're getting, I'm not such a *metsiye*, and this was shocking too, the lapse into Yiddish, because she was the least Jewish of all the girls he knew, and it embarrassed her, that hook on her nose, which she would pay to straighten, but it corresponded to something authentic that she would reach for when nothing else would do. And he protested, of course he did, he was the grateful one, not her, we all carry darkness around inside ourselves, he too had read Dostoevsky and felt the answering chimes of rage and spleen, he too was *troubled, questioning* . . . And yes, she said, *You're sweet*, and stroked his hair, his ear, his neck, in that way which had first excited him in its raw peculiar intimacy but which he already was beginning to question, and she was saying, *You don't have the first idea*, and he already felt that she was protecting him from something, when he was the one meant to be doing the protecting, and if she was already protecting him that meant, or suggested, that there was something already missing in the world they were making together, an absence that could be filled by a dark malice, which was caused by something integral to her that she couldn't share, that he couldn't lift or reassure or orgasm away, and it wasn't until she'd alluded to some *event*, something that had transpired *long ago*, and his imagination was agog, summer camp at Seneca Lake, she dressed as a red Indian, or in tennis whites, a nymphet deflowered by a trusted family friend in a room heavy with mahogany and cigar smoke and law books, or maybe someone closer, maybe her *father* . . . ? And the most disturbing part of this was not the confession she was making, or the offer that he should cut his losses now, she would always love him, but he deserved someone better, which caused him of course to protest that *he* was the lucky one, he'd kill himself or run away to Europe if she broke their engagement, she couldn't do that to him, the worst part about it all was that as he imagined the study where the crime had taken place, he was finding himself more excited than he would choose to be, and aroused, and the comforting he was enacting—*Listen to me!*, to which she responded with, *You're sweet. Oh!*—was being presented with an urgency that he hoped had the force of truth, and so what if they were going to be late, so what if her younger sister would smirk when she saw them, so what if her father so obviously hated him for what he was doing with the daughter, that had caused them to be late for dinner, in the pursuit of that pleasure, that duty, that, maybe, he had first trained her into.

For summer jobs, Emma had worked as a waitress for a company that catered big events in Catskills resorts and in the yacht clubs of Long Island, and it was at one of those that she had met her future husband.

Her friend Nell had reported sick with food poisoning (it was the shrimps, she said; it was the whiskey sours, Emma knew, mixed by a manufacturer of sunglass frames who had taken her out to sea on a fibreglass boat named for the manufacturer's absent wife, Lucille) so Emma had agreed, for an extra twenty bucks, to model leisurewear by the hotel pool. She had to stand by sun loungers and deck tables where families centred around their men, these endless men with their grey chest hair and their heavy tanned bellies and their too-short shorts, sucking at cocktails through straws and sitting astride their loungers, leaning forward to stuff burgers into their mouths, catching the drips of ketchup and mustard on paper plates and white napkins with their oh-so-capable hands, engineers' hands, manufacturers' hands, the hands that can twist spectacle frames into shape, that slap rear ends in elevators, at hotel bars, that can, as if somehow avuncular, slide a finger between bikini strap and skin to inflict further bruising.

This modelling of leisurewear is less demeaning than waitressing. She goes from table to table, she stands a little apart, dreamy, she holds the pose as she has been instructed to do, hips jutting to the side, one foot turned outwards, almost first position, and she slides her hands down her body, which was the gesture that she hadn't been able to make the first times without giggling, but now she does it almost without thinking, hands nearly touching body, which is what excites these men, these Lesters and Bruces and Joes, which is what annoys these women, these Lucilles and Harriets and Lilas, the men make their remarks which slide past her, and the women try not to look furious, and she extends the conversations, to appease the Lucilles, to put the transaction with the Lesters on a professional footing, and she gets a bonus from any sale, which she has promised to split with Nell.

So she stands there, jutting, slowly showing the lines of the swimsuit summer dress and they make their remarks, and this time there is no sale but they won't let her go until they have agreed on the colour of the dress. They ask her and she says *Green* but that isn't sufficient.

'Emerald maybe,' says one.

'Forest.'

'*Sherwood* forest?'

'I think it's just forest.'

'Racing green.'

And it goes on, these names of colours, these shades of green, offered and discarded because none of them is quite accurate, until the fattest one, who is wearing a modesty cover of a pale linen shirt over his soft chest and thrusting belly, finally looks up from his burger and examines her with cold appraisal, and pronounces the single word *Lime* with absolute authority and returns to his eating. And they clap their hands as if this is a performance from a prodigy, and say *Les always knows* . . . Now she is released, to go to the next table where she will display herself to someone almost as out of place as herself, a nephew out from the city on his break from his medical studies to visit family, and the look he gives her is of utter desire and longed-for complicity, and she feels, for maybe the first time in her life, seen.

They honeymooned in Europe, an itinerary put together by a travel agent his mother knew, who allowed them three days in Paris, two in Rome, two on the Amalfi coast including a last day in Capri where it rained, and throughout they seemed to be doing more travelling than sight-seeing, even though their legs were tired and they gratefully soaked their feet each night before dinner as much as the peculiar plumbing would allow; there was more time occupied at airports and in taxi cabs and checking in and checking out, where he tipped generously as his father had trained him to do, and the locals all seemed to despise him for it. They saw the Mona Lisa over the shoulders of a tour group of Germans, they waited in line for hours before they were permitted to twist their necks to witness the Michelangelo ceiling in the Sistine chapel, which, yes, was glorious, but also smaller than he had expected. She looked elegant, *chic*, she wore a headscarf in Italy, and dark glasses, which she liked to keep on even in the dim light of Campari bars and churches, there was a soaring quality to her, even in the stillest of moments, lighting candles for her sister and her lost brother in a church in Rome, shielding the flame against the Renaissance breeze, maybe saying a prayer but he couldn't hear because he was standing a little away, to give her space for her gestures and her grief, and how beautiful she was, and he marvelled that she knew so instinctively and well what *to do*, the awkward smile as she backed out of the church, as she adjusted the headscarf, as she told him to give two lira to the custodian at the door, which of course was the right thing to do, even if there was no clear instruction to do so.

So that's what these glossy magazines teach you, he said, wondering if there was some witchery, whether, despite the gaps, even with the Italian she had from a Dante course she'd taken one semester, there was something that connected her to these people and it was to do with the wildness of her, not despite it.

One evening, it might have been in a neighbourhood restaurant in Trastevere, where they waited with locals for an hour to gain admission to a brightly lit room where there was no menu (he had asked for it, repeatedly, in his Fodor's travel guide Italian, and they had ignored him), and you ate what you were served and it was, he supposed, *marvellous,* as she said, but his feet hurt and he was tired of waiting and tired of marvelling—at ceilings and paintings and pasta and her own instinct for soaring, the way she knew what to do, how even though she barely carried any money, except for the emergency fund he had pressed upon her (because who knows what might happen? a crowded street, a separation, the violence of Europe, she needed her passport with her at all times, and sufficient cash to pay a taxi driver to take her to the American consulate), people responded to something in her that they didn't trouble themselves to look for in him, a gaiety, a lightness along with the weight that she perpetually carried.

She told him once, several years into their marriage, when she was pregnant with Little Nicky, that he should stop punishing her. He had thought this accusation so unfair that it had almost brought him to sudden tears, *Punish you? I'm trying to look after you!* and she had interrupted him and there was a harsh crack in her voice that hadn't been there before, and she had said, so wearily, as if this was spoken from centuries ago, *You don't have to punish me, I can do a much better job of it myself* . . . He didn't know how to take this, *You want a divorce?* To this suggestion that surprised both of them, she had nodded with a daring little smile on her face, and he knew that she was trying something out, there was no sincerity in this conversation, at least from her side, and then she had laughed with her brittle laugh and asked him to fetch a pickled cucumber from the refrigerator, because his mother had told them about all the dietary obsessions she had suffered from when she was pregnant with Nicholas, and Emma had tried to go along with it, like someone who had fallen into the wrong place, come to the wrong house, with the wrong host, doing her best to accept the wrong sort of hospitality, and said, *Don't listen to me, my hormones are running amok.*

They threw a Spring Party and then a Summer Party and then an Autumn Party where everything was russet and bronze and a little band set up in the television corner of the living room and played Autumn Leaves. And they had decided this is what they would do, throw a seasonal party four times a year, it would keep them up to date with their obligations, everyone who had invited them to a supper party or for a weekend upstate would have their hospitality satisfactorily repaid, and they could invite his friends from the hospital, and the medical boards, and the new literary and artistic friends she was making and all those neighbourhood women she couldn't quite bear but knew she had to tolerate, *Darling if you had to listen to her you'd hate her too* . . . And then the seasonal parties became twice-a-year parties, annual Summer and Winter parties that she and he, despite the glamour, their allure that had everyone longing to attend, the status an invitation bestowed, came to dread.

They no longer hired a band. And nor was she responsible

for preparing the food, but she had to supervise *everything*, the caterers and the menu and the flowers, and the blue jeans and black roll necks of the serving staff (and how he failed to emulate the little pep talk she gave them before the party began on those few occasions when he was allowed to substitute for her), and the cleaners who came before and the cleaners who came after, *because Betty isn't really capable of the heavy lifting, I should probably let her go, but she cleaned for my mother and I don't know where else she'd go, she needs the money, her homelife is such a worry*, and the glassware and the wine and the cocktails, which he no longer mixed, they had a bartender for that, brought in from the Carlyle, and somehow this created more work for her, which created anxiety for him, he couldn't relax behind the party smile that he'd practised so hard to make believable, having to lift away full ashtrays that were balancing on knees and about to tip their contents on to the sofa, *Let me have that, sport*, and *Why don't we discuss that at the hospital?* and flirting with the wrong people out of a strange kind of absent-mindedness that might lead to severe consequences, and *Nicky! You should be in bed!* as Little Nicky watched rapt at these events as if they were stretching into his own future.

Occasionally, mother and son would take an unscheduled walk at night, to pick something up from the deli, or just to be in the city together, and she would hold Nicky's hand tight, maybe a little too fiercely. She made him walk in the lee of the apartment buildings, under canopies, swerving around doormen, around basement service staircases where hard men in blue shirts lounged smoking. He wanted a shirt like that, soft pack of cigarettes in the pocket, pens and pencils, his name stitched in red. If he tried to move around, away from the buildings, she tugged him fiercely back again, bravely taking the middle of the sidewalk for herself, protecting her son from the object that would one day fall from the sky.

All of them acting like ingenues and juvenile leads, looks designed to smoulder across the punch bowl, her hidden depths, his reserves of passion, the tragedies that blight me that, with your love, I shall overcome . . . widowed mothers, those dark places of childhood, a house on the cliff, wild stallions in the field, lightning strikes the single tree, my hands on your shoulders, yours grip my waist, and once we could do this dance together, but our steps don't quite synchronise and neither will our memories, and anxious hands push us back towards the middle of the room, protecting the bottles, the punch bowl, the glassware, our dignities, and yes, a slower kind of dance would be the safer choice now, and I need not wear a girdle like some of these aging ingenues here, and let me rest my cheek here, my head on your shoulder, clasp me tight, don't worry about the looks upon us, my doctor husband, your dipso wife, my stubborn child, these our friends and cousins and children and nemeses, is this what we studied at Harvard and Columbia and Vassar for, to be in this swaying room on Riverside Drive on a winter night in 1969, the cynosure of all their eyes?

There were other storylines at their parties, it was not just the hostess dancing too close with a doctor who was not her husband. There's Leo who longs for other men but outside of these parties is too timid to do much more than slow his steps when he walks past certain movie houses on 42nd Street, which maybe he finally would enter one day, but it will take the intercession of another, a knowing angel will have to extend a hand, and every party, even the most depressingly familiar one, is opportunity for this to happen, and there's Leo lingering by the bar, talking to the younger of the barmen dressed in blue jeans and black turtleneck, and Leo's wife's diet pills are fuelling something, his hair falling away from the shape he bruises it into before leaving his house, coaxing it not to fall, not to reveal the baby pinkness of his scalp, but his hair now is wild, and Leo's hands comb through it, disarraying it even more and he laughs, he is a temptress, one of those tragic heroines he analyses with his students at P.S. 135, Cleopatra, the jewelled serpent of the Nile, or Blanche Dubois, longing for the enlivening kindness, so please, young man, just refill this glass and pop a second maraschino cherry on top, there is so much we can say to one another, so much that you might teach me.

Doctor Husband watching her, those eyes that go down such a storm at the hospital, but despite the messages they send, he is not all-knowing, he knows almost nothing, least of all himself; he is not all-forgiving, he forgives nothing, especially not the slights upon him, or the weaknesses or appetites of others, which to him, so grave, are the same phenomenon, he is as frightened as Leo, except Leo is not frightened now, Leo is no longer Blanche Dubois—*switch*—he is Byron's Don Juan, the youthful hero, striding through life, whom everyone adores, whose youthful bravado makes all women love him, all men want to be him, and all boys want to be his helper, his loyal companion, his aide-de-camp in his campaigns, his ardent journey through fate.

And Leo's wife would take him home, and maybe he would be permitted some ceremony tonight, and the turtlenecked boys will pack up and go on to a bar they liked to go to, because this was just the work part of the evening, and attentions from the likes of Leo, and Janice, whose husband's hands were now doing things that are both annoying and irresistible, were just part of the conditions of their job, there may be an anecdote to tell later on, but essentially this was the dead time of day, when nothing really happened, just earning money to pay the rent and mix another drink for a rich old person.

Emma didn't realise how lonely it was for him. He longed to help her, why couldn't she give him credit for that! He did not become a doctor just so his mother could take a photograph of his bronze name plaque outside his office and show it to her friends on bridge nights, *It's on Park Avenue, the good Park, near the museums* . . . he had a vocation, a calling, Galen, Hippocrates, Jenner, Lister, Pasteur, Schweitzer, Sawyer . . . of course Doctor Sawyer was no paragon of virtue, he was human after all, there were certain benefits, women patients grateful for what he does, and yes, sometimes he succumbed. Things recently had become complicated with Mary, his nurse, but none of this is *against* Emma, she pushes him away emotionally even while reaching for him physically, why can't she see that he needs a little kindness too . . .

Leo's wife was on Nicholas's arm, Nicholas clasped her hand while detaching it, he might have fallen a little behind with some of the peer research in the gastroenterology field, but here was something that Park Avenue had taught him, how to end the clasp without causing offence, reassuring the woman, even to some extent flattering her, while ending the contact, *No, we mustn't: think of our obligations, our standing, our spouses, our children* . . . And there was Nicky, again so soft and goggle-eyed at the door, *creeping* around, it's something he gets from his mother, that sidewaysness, unable to enter a room in any straightforward motion, and anyway he should be in bed, and why hadn't Emma put him there? Instead so busy being pawed by Roy.

Come on, sport! he said, in that gruff loving tone that he had longed for as a child and so wished someone had used with him, and even if he had to exert a little force to bring his son away, he felt the connection deepen between them in this moment.

The following day, most of the party cleared away, the breakages accounted for, the first thank you cards and apologies beginning to arrive, they take a walk in Riverside Park. Nicky runs to the playground in that stuttering old man way of his, his movements an apology for his arrival, that's what the doctor doesn't like about his son, there is something *sneaky* about him. And even this urgency to get to the swings has the air of performance about it.

'The boy lacks sincerity,' he says.

This could go either way. Be taken as wisdom, a dry meaningful aphorism that brings them together, reminding them both of their one truly shared project, or else she might despise him for it, say he's been talking to Leo and *that* crowd again, being a literary man doesn't really suit you, dear heart.

Doctor Sawyer. The name doesn't really suit either of them. There is too much of a whiff of General Hospital about it. She uses her maiden name, Hoffman, as her writing name, which she claims is a way of protecting him, when he takes it as a further pushing away. His grandfather had arrived from pogrom Europe with the name Seger and quickly changed it and Nicholas sometimes wishes he had the gumption to change it back, but that would require too many explanations, too much administration, all his memberships, his business cards, the Park Avenue plaque. When they had met, she had loved to call him that, *Doctor Seger, dear heart* . . . with a wide-eyedness about it, so tentative as if afraid of being about to break something . . . So this is how people feel, we're making something here, the stuff of popular song and lyric poetry, and it may not be the opera I was expecting, and dreading, but there's something to be said for the manufactured pop song, its reliability, its form that we know so well, time for the chorus again now, but instead it's still at the bridge, which seems to go on forever . . .

She just nods. Nicky waves at them from the swing and he waves back, and she automatically says, *Careful now!*, and the day is unseasonably warm but still she huddles inside her clothes.

But when they meet someone they know, Nina Weiss, who lives on West End Avenue, whose husband is a shrink, and who is training to be something, an art therapist maybe, and who, Emma says, always flirts with Nicholas, which Nicholas denies, but secretly he thinks so too, Emma sparks back into the self she presents most appropriately in this place, at this hour, in this light.

She sparkles. It is as if the real Emma, good Emma, has returned, and while he might resent that it takes an outsider to find her, nonetheless he is relieved that she is back. Bad Emma, distanced, dislocated, cold Emma frightens him.

It is at moments like this that she dazzles. This is not only Good Emma, this is Best Emma. She delights him, alarms him, the connections her mind makes. When she writes novels or short stories there can be something forced about the outcome. It is always accomplished, and polished, but there isn't the life in it that is to be found in her conversation which is where her genius finds its fullest expression. It's like listening to jazz, but not the free-form stuff in which the listener is the performer's victim, condemned to applaud wherever whim and virtuosity take them; here the listener is equal, part of the show, a spontaneous interaction, your self, my self, this place, your idea, our breaths, her fancy, her imagination, this sunshine, my ears, her kindness, her *generosity*, she is embodying something, giving flight to a shared endeavour. This can't happen without us, and it can't happen without us being here, in this very place, *now*.

Except, now, in this moment, it falters. And this is no judgment on her, but on Nina Weiss, who, bafflingly, resists the performance, the show, the connection. She doesn't smile when she should, when she must, when Emma does a riff on Mike and Mel's poodle. Nina doesn't offer him a complicity of smile or look or touch him on the arm, the lightest glide that suggests so much, were things different, were they *free*. Even when she is asked about Bobby and Janet, that safest of topics, her prodigious children, whose many talents demand limitless applause, their breathtaking futures, her responses are restrained, barely more than cordial.

'We didn't see you at the party,' he finally says.

They were getting nowhere, Emma's skills had failed. Better he take this over, that gruff directness that serves him so well in his consulting room, there is a time and place for ornament and arabesques, but a straight line is the quickest way between two points. No one voluntarily misses their parties. Sometimes he wonders quite why they are so highly regarded, if maybe they disappoint but some group mind had elected to pretend otherwise. It was Emma, it must be Emma, she authors them, and how we long for the license she grants to her characters.

Next time, he tells himself, he will relax more, drink more, forget those responsibilities of the host, trust the staff, his wife, maybe even himself. It can't be entirely without him that these things occur. He is the tether that allows Emma's balloon to soar, and maybe he too possesses some of those qualities of lightness.

He hasn't shaved this morning. He often doesn't shave on a Sunday, and now maybe he would allow the beard and moustache that Emma has forbidden him to grow unimpeded. As if she is thinking the same thought, and sometimes they do think the same thought, she raises a faltering hand to her own cheek.

If Nina hadn't come that means that there is a grudge. Had he misjudged the *flirting*? Is there a problem with Barry? He doubts that to be the case. Barry is always cheerful. He can't picture him as a jealous husband aroused by some innocent social play. Little Nicky? A crime in the schoolyard? Children fall out with each other all the time, and then back in again. There would be nothing there that could carry a grudge into the adult world. Emma then. Emma had done something, said something. He takes her hand as if he might prevent her from causing further damage, and also, he thinks, here is an expression of solidarity. Despite the divisions, those missed rhythms, we stand together.

Nina Weiss purses her mouth tightly shut. And opens it again.

'I promised Barry I would not be speaking about this,' she says.

She looks over to the play area for deliverance. Janet sits on the bench with Little Nicky. Bobby is in the sandpit.

'Look after your brother young lady!' Nina calls over, and Janet gives her the most cursory of nods, doesn't look up from the task, the things she is arranging on the bench that she and Nicky are rapt by.

'You didn't see me because I wasn't at the party,' Nina says.

'Is something wrong?' Emma says.

There is sickness in the background, a father who had never recovered from being at war, a mother with something internal, ovarian cysts? It can't be money worries, being a shrink is a license to print money.

'Barry?' Nicholas says.

'Have we done something to offend you?' Nina says.

There is a gulp in her voice as if she is pushing back tears.

'Of *course* not!' Emma says.

'We weren't at your party because you didn't invite us to your party.'

And, before either of them has a chance to react, she has gone to the sand pit and swooped up Bobby and taken Janet by the hand, who is so shocked at this peremptory intrusion into a world her mother had no rights of access to, that she doesn't even lift her voice in protest and despite her outrage she allows herself to be dragged away, Little Nicky gathering the items that have fallen in the process, four metal jacks and a blue rubber ball that rolls away from him and which he has to scamper after and crawl for despite the dust that gathers on to his legs and shorts, despite his mother calling after him to behave like a *human being*, and Nina has gone and her children have gone, and after they have retrieved Nicky and wiped some of the worst of the debris from him, his voice squeaks at his mother's fingernails scratching his dusty skin, and it is not until they are half-way home themselves that they find the liberty to consider what they have just heard.

How many other invitations might have gone astray? Were there other notable absences? Which invitation list did she use? (Because it is one of her duties to fill out all the addresses herself.) Might he have dropped one of the cards en route? (Because it is one of his duties to take the envelopes and deliver them, a fun activity that he takes Nicky on, and how they enjoy walking their streets with purpose, men with a mission, handing cards to apartment building doormen, taking the out-of-town ones to the Post Office.)

'I remember delivering it,' he says. 'I gave it to their doorman myself.'

Or did he?

'Did you write the invitation?' he says.

'I must have, mustn't I? if you remember delivering it. You do remember delivering it?'

Does he actually remember giving it to Tony? Maybe Nicky had done that, he has some memory of the doorman saying, *Hey soldier!*, and being able to hit some rough accord with his son that he has never been able to find.

'I think so.'

'You think so.'

And Nicky had asked afterwards about names, why children and doormen and barbers mostly have names that end with y, whereas parents never do.

'I mean yes, I think so.'

Now they suspect each other, and themselves, sideways glares as they go into their own building, to be greeted by their own doorman, Tommy, who says, *Doctor Sawyer, Mrs Sawyer*, and then, giving his customary crisp salute to Nicky, *How you doing champ?*

Nicholas asks if there is any mail for them that they'd neglected to pick up during the week, no returned letters for example, and Tommy moves briskly to the little room the building calls the office, which is where everyone knows they store a fifth of whisky to warm them at night, to keep that subservient affability topped up to its constant level, and once Nicholas had returned in the small hours, a conference in Indianapolis, missed connections, a final taxi ride from Kennedy at three in the morning, and Tommy was a little slow to emerge from the office, and he had looked shy and rumpled and Nicholas had wondered if that had been the smell of *marijuana* clinging to him. This time he returns with just a flyer for orthopaedic supports that Nicholas crumples up and tosses into the ashtray by the elevator.

There are rumours in the neighbourhood—the Weisses hadn't been invited because of the affair that Nicholas was having with Nina. The Weisses hadn't been invited because of the affair that Emma was having with Barry. The Weisses *had* been invited but hadn't come because of the affair Nicholas was having with Nina. And so forth. They hadn't been invited because of some other, even more sinister reason. They had been invited but hadn't come because that sinister reason. (And hadn't there been another notable absentee? A couple more notable absentees?)

Nicholas and Emma stopped discussing the question. It had become tired, no longer amusing, not at all amusing. They sit in bed, Emma with those half-moon glasses she has adopted, a legal pad balanced on top of a square of wood she calls her writing block. She does her writing, what she calls her *work*, often at night now, which does prompt a number of questions, such as, What does she do all day? She has a woman for the cleaning and a woman for the ironing, his own mother had no such aids, but here she is, half-loaded from vodka cocktails and who knows what else, in her baby doll nightdress that it would be an impertinence, an affront, an *assault* for him to touch, with her writing pad and writing block, and the jokes that they used to share are no longer funny, and maybe that is because they don't share them anymore.

He knows that Emma has stopped taking Little Nicky down to the swings on West End Avenue. She says that the playground on Riverside is just as good, better even, and in this weather, who needs the walk. They seem never to bump into the Weisses anymore. Barry seldom comes to the Wednesday night poker game. They don't seem to cross at Zabars or the Thalia.

'Don't you think . . . ?'

'Think what?'

He had been expecting to have to repeat himself to attract her attention. But she has allowed him her attention immediately. There is that dangerous look she gets when she's drunk too much vodka.

'I don't know,' he says.

He had been about to say, *think that we should make everything right with the Weisses?*

There had been one night at the card game when he and Barry had both been in attendance and nothing felt really wrong, everything happened much as it usually did, Jerry wore his stupid hat, Mat got most of everyone's money, the same food was eaten, the same jokes made, but the evening had broken up earlier than it usually did, and it had been as if everyone was performing their roles rather than living them and showing the *strain* of it all.

'You know,' she says to him one night, 'Nina had a party?'

'What do you mean?' he says, knowing perfectly well what the words mean, and the emotion she is feeling while saying them, and the likelihood that she has known this for some time and been unable to speak the sentence, not so much because of the emotion she would be feeling when saying it, but because she would have been unable to find quite the right tone for it, the lightness of register, the opportunity to share in a little mockery of their friend, her existential amusement at everything, a superiority that doesn't present as arrogance.

'A party,' she says. 'Can you believe it?'

And it is not that Nina had a party that is so surprising, although he can't remember the last time the Sawyers went to a Weiss party, because one of the points of being the great hostess of the Upper West Side is that she has to parcel out her own attendance at others' affairs. He has never quite grasped the rules of this. She will attend the dreariest charity functions, the dumbest art show, but when it came to parties thrown by their *friends*, she has these obscure rules that not only would she never explain, but she would deny even having them. What is surprising, unthinkable, impossible, is that they hadn't been invited to it.

'Are you sure?' he says.

This does not require or deserve a response so it doesn't receive it. What has upset her so much is the disloyalty of those who attended.

'I'd like to see a guest list.'

'So you can do what? Take reprisals?'

She has the grace and the self-consciousness to laugh at this, but he wonders if that is what she does intend.

Emma wants to punish Nina, and she would like to punish everyone who attended her stupid party.

When he sees Barry it is clear that whatever is going on it is between their wives. Neither of them would ever be disloyal but all the same they're civilised men, it would be a shame if they had to fall out over this. It shouldn't tear at the fabric of their lives.

She has taken to sleeping a lot during the day, which means she is sleepless at night. Her husband stirs beside her as she gets up to eat ice cream and smoke cigarettes and watch the Late Late Show on Channel 2 and she both loves and detests the titles, the lights going out in the cartoon city, the jaunty music, her own movie house, mint chocolate chip.

Her routine has changed. She hears them talking about her. Doctor Madrigal upped her medication but that doesn't seem to help. Nicholas tells her to take the *long view*: just because she doesn't think it is helping doesn't mean that it is not helping.

'But that's like me saying my lucky penny has saved the world from atomic warfare.'

'It's not at all. That's—'

And she hears him swallow the words *crazy thinking* . . .

'. . . superstition,' he says.

'But you can't prove it's not the case,' she says, and she was always good at this, captain of debate team, she could take any proposition and build a logical argument from it, a perfect unassailable structure. They told her she could become anything she wanted to be, an ambassador's wife or even a lawyer herself. And instead she had married young because she liked having sexual intercourse with the cocksure young man he had been—and even that wasn't quite true, she liked the prospect of sexual intercourse, the idea of it, sometimes the aftermath, the reality of it occurring with Doctor Nicholas Sawyer turned out not to be what she had been after at all.

'It is perfectly likely that your meds have been helping, a lot.'

'*Perfectly likely*,' she says. 'Isn't that a tautology?'

'Tautology,' he says.

'Yes, that's what I said,' Emma says.

They decide not to hold their customary Summer Party. Neither mentions it, but the time passed when she would have been writing out the invitation cards and planning the menus and securing the help. The punch bowl they always have as a centrepiece at their summer parties stays downstairs in the building's basement storage, beside the samovar they use in winter. Neither of them mentions the party, its absence, although Nicky does.

'You guys not having a party this summer?' he says, and she wonders at this, the way that their rhythms have probably structured so much of what he would come to think of as *his*, of *himself*, he'd probably be talking to his shrink about this in years to come, the time his parents didn't throw their summer party, or the time that his parents stopped throwing parties at all. And when did he start talking like this, *You guys . . . ?*

'We won't be having a summer party this year,' she tells people.

Sometimes she blames Nicholas's work. Sometimes she blames Nicholas. Treacherously, she implies a darkness there, an instability.

'He's been working so hard,' she says.

A consequence of this is that people seem to think that the Sawyers are throwing their customary party but that she has decided not to invite *them*. She catches the flight of this rumour, as it passes through the playground, the Upper West Side, it reaches her standing outside Little Nicky's school gates.

There is nothing she can say to disprove it. It is like her lucky penny and the atom bomb. The more she announces that they would not be holding their summer party, the more it seems to take root that the party has shrunk, become more select, and *Who does she think she is . . . ?*

She thinks maybe they should hold it, or a version of it after all. Bring the punch bowl up from storage, see who is around, make things more spontaneous, like they used to be. This is what they need, a celebration of the season, all cultures have a festival of lights in wintertime, observe the solstice in summer, renewal celebrated with family and friends. They have allowed their lives, their marriage, to become too routinised, too formal. This is what we put in Nicky's lunch sandwiches, tuna salad alternating daily with peanut butter and jelly, except on Mondays when they are built out of the leftovers of Sunday lunch. This is how we announce our willingness for intercourse (hard to call it desire any more, it's an alleviation, a proxy for something else). We won't write out names on cards, it will be relaxed, intimate, *cosy*.

It is impossible. The first people she invites, the same look of malicious supposition greets her invitation. They think that she has had more rejections than usual this year, *and who would be surprised at that!*, and that she is now issuing late invitations from her B-list, from her C-list, to bump up the numbers, to fill the apartment, to crowd away the shame of absence. They all apologise, with a formal indirectness, and make excuses, or say they'll have to consult their diaries, even those who have never been invited before, but they think they might have a *thing* on that night, and such a shame, they'd so love to come, the Sawyers' summer party is legendary, such a highlight of the season, so sorry to miss it this year . . .

She even, maybe in desperation, maybe as an act of reconciliation, invites Nina Weiss.

We weren't going to have it this year, she says and waits for the malice of supposition to reveal itself, but what Nina is showing is beyond coldness. So guarded, and this is her friend. Had been her friend. Which casts into doubt any of the relationships she takes for granted. Any of her friends. Who is to say this is my friend? Who is to say this is my father? (How, after all, can I ever truly know?) Who is to say this is my husband? Mightn't they have planted a simulacrum of him? I can't believe in this one; he is too disappointing, too rigid, too *alien* to be the man I thought I was marrying. Maybe the switch had taken place then at the wedding, all that time ago . . . This was all guff about *growing apart*: something inorganic like a husband-simulacrum is not capable of growing at all. And who is to say this is my child? He doesn't look like me. I don't recognise anything about him. He doesn't even resemble himself. And who is to say this is my doorman? He acts like my doorman but all those other doormen act like my doorman. *Hold my hand Nicky. I don't care how old you are. And no, stay close to the buildings.*

They are in the line for the deli counter. Nina had got there first and Emma would not have stayed in line had she seen Nina ahead of her, but her hair is different, it is cut shorter and is a slightly lighter shade, redder. It catches the overhead light and lifts away from her nape when she takes a step forward, closer to the counter. She suddenly turns and Emma may not look away or walk away because that would be an admission of defeat, as if Nina has greater right to this place than she does, so Emma shines out a smile, perhaps one slightly more brilliant than the moment demands, and she takes a half-step forward and it is hard not to feel gratified that Nina takes an inadvertent step in retreat and collides with the rear of the woman waiting ahead of her. The ensuing apologies allow Emma the opportunity to relax her smile. She waits, demure, ready for anything, and when Nina has disentangled from the woman in front, and the line has taken a further group step forward, so that there is only one matron now between Nina and the counter, the two women who had once been friends look at each other again.

The correct course of action now, Emma has written about it herself in her own magazine etiquette column, would be for Nina to yield her place to the customer that separates her from Emma—Emma may not join her, that would be committing the solecism of jumping the line. But Nina does not yield her place. She smooths down her coat as if to wipe away any memory of the recent collision. She tries smiling. She juts out her chin and finds a more successful smile this time.

'Emma,' she says.

'Nina,' says Emma.

'I've been meaning . . .'

'*So* much.'

Irritation emanates from the woman between them. This is partly due to the customer currently at the counter, who is showing signs of being there for significantly longer than is her right, rethinking herself, asking for changes to her order, more lox, less tongue. But it is largely due to being talked over, and through, by Emma and Nina.

'Lady,' says the woman. Although she says it to the floor so it is unclear whether it is directed at Nina or Emma or to the customer at the counter.

'How is Bobby?' Emma says—and after Nina's report, which Emma barely hears, but is able to nod and smile not too brilliantly, and relax her hold on her shopping bag, which she has become aware she is gripping too tight, and before there can be a retaliation in kind, she says,

'And how's Janet?'

Again, the report. The woman at the counter is about to settle up and pay before she remembers she had forgotten she wants pepper salami. The woman in between mutters and sighs and this distracts Nina, which gives Emma a further gap to say,

'And Barry. How *is* Barry?'

Thereby demonstrating, or implying, a shared knowledge, the thing that afflicts him, because there is always a thing afflicting Barry, who had been over-cossetted in youth, and who falls prey to anything going around, any current infection physical or psychic, which Nina has to nurse him through and once, in a rare moment of utter honesty, admitted to Emma how much she despises her husband.

They move forward again and Nina is at the front of the line and is reading out from a list a much larger order than Emma has ever heard her make. And then she is done and Emma is telling her about Nicky, and she takes a step forward, and here is the moment when in former times they would be deciding on where to go for coffee, or maybe an impromptu walk down to the Guggenheim or the Frick. They make no such arrangement for coffee. Emma does not enquire why Nina has bought so much today at the deli counter. Nor, as she might have done, does she suggest a reason that protects them both, a social for the parents in Janet's class maybe, which would not include Emma and therefore does not exclude her.

'We weren't going to be having our summer party this year,' Emma says.

An eyebrow rises in response, which Emma knows is her own gesture mimicked unconsciously back at her. There had been a year when every woman on the Upper West Side had been practising their Emmaisms.

'But,' she continues, 'maybe we should. Would you—'

She doesn't know how to say it. She has issued so many

invitations over the years, graciously, flatteringly, imploringly, drily, imperiously, cursorily, importantly, off-handedly, whimsically, confidentially . . . but the tone appropriate to this moment is lost to her.

She is floundering and the worst part of this is that Nina *feels sorry* for her, they had all been invested in her eminence, their own self-worth had been bound up in their estimation of her value.

It is her turn at the counter, Nina nudges her attention towards it and mercifully this moment is over, Emma can issue her brisk commands that demonstrate her undeniable good taste and status along with a clear respect for the deli counterman's craft. *How are your parents, Jose?*

When this is over, her meats and cheeses wrapped in oiled paper, stacked inside her bag, and a piece of strudel for her husband, the ingredients for a birthday cake for her son, and she is at the door again, slipping on her sunglasses against the sun, against the world, its harshness, wondering if maybe she should take her first bloody mary of the day right now. She could try morning drinking for a while, see where that leads. She needs something to take the place of her writing, which never gets done any more, leaving an empty space, separate from mothering and wifing and neighbouring, which she could fill with liquor.

On the threshold, there is an awkward comedy with a new customer coming in, neither of them in tune to the other's movements, they keep impeding one another so the other may not come in and Emma may not go out. She wonders if there is decision at the bottom of this, she feels safer here, she might settle in this world, she could find tasks to justify her presence here, there is probably space out back, where they might put a bed up for her, here she could sleep when at rest from her duties, or perhaps pass her allegiance to one of these men, Jose or Mikey or Antonio himself, all of them dark with black hair like wire across their arms, down their chests from their throats, she might find a protector here, at little cost to herself.

There is a can of olives at the bottom of the bag, which she has taken, on a barely noticeable whim. Maybe that is the way forward, fill her days with theft, go down to Saks, find something wildly unsuitable to steal, another trophy of the day.

Things tremble. She can see the vibrating edges of objects that she had previously assumed to be stable. Lines are liquid, everything shimmers as if just about to dissolve. Planes she had previously thought to be solid are, she discovers, made of light ready to merge. For so long she had assumed things were fixed, but they are not, it is all pure unstable energy on the point of collapse. She must feel things, answer this all with a stern corrective of the physical. The prod into her back from the customer behind her impatient to leave the store. The tapping of the sole of her mule as she moves from linoleum to the ridge of metal in the doorway, to the smoothness of the sidewalk. The sight of discarded cigarette ends, chewing gum, the trails of pigeon mess. A dog barks. A man shouts. The sound of car horns. The smell of pastry freshly baked. Her shoe's *blueness*, even if that shimmers along with everything else—by concentrating on the physical particular she might block out the instability of everything else.

She had not thought that Nina would be waiting outside for her. Emma adjusts her sunglasses, her grip on her shopping bag. It is a triumph to compose her features into an expression appropriate to this day without further provoking the world into collapse.

'I wanted to say—is something wrong?' Nina says.

Emma chuckles brightly in response. 'Nothing is wrong,' she says. 'Except maybe everything. Kidding! Just kidding ok.'

Nina looks doubtfully at her. Cunningly Emma lifts her sunglasses an iota so she may look down at her shoes without being observed to be doing so and to be secured by the fullness of their colour. *My shoes are blue!* she wants to say, but does not, and this withholding is an act of consideration rather than selfishness. Nina will have to come to this truth on her own, in her own way, like a pilgrim reaching the shrine, or a patient whose analysis is soon to be over; we all must discover our own truths, which is why being a parent is so desperately hard, and in some cases, her own for example, lonely.

'We're having a party,' Nina says.

There is nothing to say to that. Emma lowers her sunglasses, shifts her shopping bag from one hand to the other to relieve the strain on her skin, the lines that the handles had been cutting into her palms, but then she misses the sensation of that and transfers the bag back again.

'You've probably heard,' Nina says. 'I don't know what's happening, I really don't, but you're my friend and I treasure our friendship and I hope you'll be able to come to our party.'

Has she really said that she treasures their friendship? She must have planned this speech while waiting for Emma to be finished at the counter. Emma wonders what words have been selected against, chosen for a moment and then discarded.

'Cherish our friendship,' she says.

'Yes,' Nina says and deciding, despite a certain thickness in Emma's tone, that this statement is made in the same spirit as her offering. 'I do too.'

'Friendship and love,' Emma says maybe too primly.

And now Nina is becoming a little unsure, perhaps unnerved. Their spot on the sidewalk is precarious (and one day Nina will realise that everything is precarious, a revelation that Emma would like to protect her from); it is too close to the delicatessen door and they have to keep swaying out of people's paths into the deli and out and along the sidewalk to the north and to the south, and there are people darting through to cross the road, and those who are going to the newspaper stand for cigarettes and gum and newspapers, and maybe this would be Emma's spot, when she is not at her place in the back of the deli, under the protection of one of those black-wired men, her sexual *favours* would be sufficient to hold her place there, and in the day she would be here, on the sidewalk, buffeted as if by the wind. There is the question of food, of meals, but presumably in the economy of the deli, food is cheap, and there would be many scraps, mistakes made at the meat slicer, tomatoes that are slightly too irregular for the fastidious customer's salad.

'So, we're having a party, and we'd love it if you came, it's on Saturday. We'd love it for you and Nick to be there. You should have had an invitation already, but just in case you haven't I'll send Bobby out to deliver one.'

This is all so perfect. She had underestimated Nina. She doesn't think this had been prepared. It is the inspiration of the moment and it touches upon community and marriage and family, and all she can do is to bow her head before it.

'Thank you,' she says knowing that she would rather die than attend this party of Nina's.

The correct thing now would be to ask after Bobby, but she might already have done that, and to touch Nina upon her arm—is that a mole there, growing silently between the freckles?—to listen to whatever small ordeal has been sent to test her family in the past few days, but the kindest thing now, for both of them, is to release her, which she does. She touches Nina on the arm, fingers shying away from the mole and that is silly, it can't be contagious, but she is getting more squeamish these days and she can't help herself, and moves forward so her cheek glides past Nina's and she says, *Thank you*, again, and puts so much sincerity and trust and half-healed regret into the words that perhaps this utterance is her masterpiece.

Her fear of hospitals is famous. She had watched her mother

die in one, and that Nicky was born in another hadn't been sufficient to bring the scales down to represent life rather than death. Her husband takes this personally, that this is a rejection of him, of his work, of his worth. Soon after Little Nicky's birth, she had spent two weeks in Bellevue, suffering from 'nervous exhaustion', 'post-partum depression'. If she had needed further evidence that hospitals were death places rather than life places, and she did not, then that would have done it.

She always crosses the street to avoid walking past the entrance of Mount Sinai in case a series of events might culminate in her being swaddled in white with her arms strapped tight and useless to her chest, and being wheeled towards the elevator while screaming, *It's not me! It's a mistake! I'm not the one!* until her mouth was filled with a gag that would hold her words down and which would be so foul-tasting that it would become a sensation that she needed.

'I think you should take him,' she says.

'I'd have to cancel patients.'

The implication from her husband is clear: *I have a job. I bring in an income. I support this place, support* you. If you're not writing any more, then the economy of the household selects you for these domestic duties, the school playground, the check-ups, the doctor, the hospital. And she does all these things, and more, the cake-bakes, the fundraisers, at least she used to. She allows her earnings to be used and ignored. All she asks in return is that he take care of anything that involves a hospital.

'You know how flustered I get in them. You know the right questions to ask. You see through it all, the snow jobs . . .'

'There are no snow jobs. These are not deceitful men. They're not trying to get more *money* out of you. They're just trying to do the right thing by their patients. And their families,' he irrelevantly adds.

She gets him to half-agree. She'll make the calls to arrange cover, just for the two hours (*maximum!*) it might take to bring Little Nicky into Mount Sinai to have his tonsils looked at.

But when it comes to it, when the day of the appointment arrives, when she is bringing Nicholas his second cup of coffee in the den, when he is dabbing his lips dry from the first, when he is straightening his cuffs and this new style he is affecting, of striped shirt and white cuffs, which she is not sure she likes, when he strokes down his unconvincing stubble, which she knows he thinks of as *magisterial* . . . he says, 'Emms? I think you're going to have to find time to take Nicky into the hospital yourself, there are some things that have come up, a consultation downtown, and Mrs Friedrich's case is developing complications . . .'

She knows that his patients depend on him, that each of his sentences is greeted as the absolute truth, but she is finding him less plausible by the day, and when he says this, as if it had all been a matter of her *time*, when he should know it's about a sheer unblinking terror, and she says, as if unpanicked, as if she could invent a preferable future merely by murmuring it, 'Yes of course, I'll take him,' because she knows that once her husband has spoken like this he is immovable, she knows that he had intended this from the outset.

Contrary to popular opinion, reality is worse than its anticipation, and anyway the two are inseparably part of the same singular horror. She is not taken away, she is not mistaken for a mental case, she is not dumped into the poor ward along with all the other lost matrons, these broken women, the estrogenal detritus of the five boroughs, dried out, used up, nuts, sedated and strapped and self-soiled . . . but the pressure of the constant possibility of this upon her, the churn upon her of the pictures her imagination invents is so extreme, and even if she knows on some ego level that this is flight or fight mechanism only, gone into overdrive, in some ways a mark of her mental health, this over-adaption to the possibility of threat makes her squeeze her son's hand too tight, in this most pathetic of fictions that she is the one comforting him.

'Mom!'

'Sorry honey,' she says.

'That hurt!'

He doesn't like being called honey or sweetheart or darling plums. He doesn't like having to hold on to her hand in public. At the supermarket he demands to be given the responsibility of directing the cart without her hand trailing it from the front, ruddering them on their way.

Nicky's outrage attracts attention, as it was designed to do.

She allows his hand to escape from hers and rests her hand on his neck, which he hates even more, the way her fingers close against the bones like a pincer. Resignedly if not quite submissively he offers his hand up again and makes her promise not to hold it too tight.

There are so many windows here, as if the reality being conducted is so horrible that they have to offer these constant reminders of outside, of elsewhere, to make it tolerable to its victims.

'Sawyer?' says the doctor who looks at Nicky's throat and who has red and yellow lollipops protruding from the pocket of his gown along with several pens and she wonders why there isn't a green one also.

'My husband,' she says. 'Nicky's father.'

'He's doing some very interesting work with lipids. I would have liked to meet him.'

And if she had made this appointment under her maiden name, which is her nom de plume? Might the doctor have said in that same tone, *Hoffman?* He won't have read her books. His wife might have. The closest he would have come is a single disapproving look at a cover by a hotel resort pool.

'But let's take a look at you sport!'

Gratifyingly, Nicky holds his hand up and waves his fingers for her to hold him when this doctor presses down on his tongue to inspect the tonsils. She takes it, delicately, gently, to comfort him, he gags from the pressure of the wooden board on his tongue and squeezes her hand frantically for her to hold his tighter, and, she wonders, what if this were to be the last time this happened? What if this were to be her last hospital visit? What if this is the last time she is to gulp with such tenderness at her son?

These last times. The last time to the supermarket. The last Friday night dinner. The last time she makes love with her husband. The joyful sense of peace after she has made her decision. She has to keep from giggling, it is such a delightful secret. Her gleeful delightful secret.

'I thought you'd given up,' he says.

'Just having this last one,' she says and this is so funny that she has to disguise her laughter as a coughing fit.

'Sorry,' she gasps. 'Not used to it.'

It would happen when the universe decides, maybe when she is about to repeat something. A repeated last time is redundant by definition.

Her last party would be at Nina's, where she will astound.

She is maybe too clever, too sparkling, too astounding. She moves at a thousand miles an hour and she thinks even faster and everything is a blur around her, of mouths and eyes, and hands reaching towards her as if to try to catch some of that energy for themselves. Nicky is staying overnight at her sister's, and she has written her letters for him, one for this birthday and one for when he is eleven and one for when he is eighteen and thirty and the ones beyond, forty-two and sixty. She has allowed herself this, these multiple last letters to Nicky, because they are all part of the same letter, which stretches over time. There is only one letter to her sister and one to her parents and one to Nicholas, which is the one she is least satisfied with, because something of her husband's pomposity spreads into her own words to him. There is no accusation or blame or even sentimentality and this is maybe what the sages mean by love.

Her one anxiety had been the question of what she is to say, what reason she is to give for leaving the party, but it doesn't matter, that is part of the joy of this, none of this matters, everything is permitted, and she is so poignantly happy, which she hopes she has been able to communicate something of in her letters. At a thousand miles an hour she takes her leave, she glides out of Nina's apartment, and down the elevator and her smiles, for the elevator man, for the doorman, *And you Tony, and you* . . . are beatific.

At her own building she enters by the basement and takes the service stairs because she does not want to inflict anything upon Tommy or the others, leave a reproach against them that they might have 'saved' her. She crouches by the door to the ninth floor corridor because there is someone, Mr Lindemann she thinks, carrying his garbage out to the compactor and she does not want to inflict upon him the thought that he might have saved her, because she has been saved, it would be impossible to explain any of this, it is like the time she and some of the girls had got high and there were truths pressing upon her but they couldn't be communicated, not in this moment, because even though they were sharing it, there had been something so personal, almost *locked in* about the sensations she had been feeling, and the next thing that had happened is that they had all been around her, stroking her arm and her face and her hair and she was unable to tell them that just because she was weeping that didn't mean that there was anything wrong.

There is nothing wrong now, everything is glorious. She climbs the stairs to the roof which is where she used to sneak up to smoke cigarettes after Nicky was born, where the building had sometimes organised drinks and cookouts, summer barbeques and cocktail nights, and there is Grant's Tomb and there the water towers of Harlem and there the river and there is New Jersey, and the world beneath her, and she takes a step and she is soaring.

2

1974

THE SECOND LETTER that he receives from his dead mother is, like the first, by his place setting at the breakfast table on the morning of his birthday.

He dreads those letters and he lives for them. Her handwriting is so heartfelt and generous that it can barely be contained by the page; even the envelopes they arrive in are ornate with the blue fountain-pen whorls of his name looping over the extent of the paper, cramping at the edges like an aviator surprised to have flown to the very limit of things. They come only on his birthdays, and only on a very few of them. The third would come on his eighteenth, the fourth on his thirtieth, the fifth on his forty-second (when he had given up expecting any more, even though they had been promised him). He anticipates each birthday in a delirium of self-reproach.

They attest to her love for him, the knowledge she has of his capacities, the joy he is capable of giving and receiving, which, she writes, are essentially the same thing. She seldom repeats herself, but there are certain things she likes to emphasise: she advises him to travel, to keep his eyes open, to be receptive to new experience, and not to judge people—unless, she jokes, he becomes a judge, in which case, it would be very appropriate to judge people.

In the weeks after his mother's death, Nicky sometimes joined his father in the den, sitting on the couch, drinking orange juice, feeling like they were two incompatible travellers thrown together by chance. Or they were undercover, a pair of scouts for an invading army who, since the demise of their loved companion, had come to detest each other more fiercely than the enemy.

His father takes his mail from the doorman when he gets back from the hospital at the end of the day, carries the pile into the den where he sips from a cut-glass tumbler of scotch on the rocks, glancing at the tv, which he calls 'the idiot box', while sorting through his correspondence.

Nicky would ask questions, Richard Nixon and Pete Rose, Spiro Agnew? what is Catfish Hunter? who is Jimmy Hoffa? what do people have against Jane Fonda? Do we like her? Should we? But his father seemed irritated by the questions, so he stopped asking them, and soon he stopped coming into his father's den, a change which went unremarked by them both. His father would return from work, take a shower, go into his den with his correspondence and whisky, *How you doing sport? How was school?* It had stopped occurring to Nicky that there could be a letter in that pile addressed to him.

Each morning his father puts out a bowl and a spoon for

him, although they take their breakfast at different times. It had used to be, in that early period after her death, that Nicky would train himself to get up early, so he might interpose himself into the rhythms of his father's day, but the effect was to irritate his father rather than create the male companionship he had been hoping for. Now he does the opposite: even if he is awake and impatient to get out of bed, and hungry for cereal, he will force himself to remain there until he hears his father about to leave, his doctor's bag clasped, keys retrieved, the clearing of the throat his father always makes as he opens the door in preparation to leave the apartment. To pass the time Nicky makes mental lists of things, places that he had gone to with his mother, some of them designated as treats—the Bronx Zoo, a magic act at Rockefeller Center—and others that were supposed to be chores, which had never felt like chores at all, accompanying his mother to collect a coat from the Garment District, where he had caught sight of the man he wanted to be; every moment with her had provided something to wonder at, even picking up cold cuts from the deli, but so many of them blur into a single trip, he can barely distinguish between them at all, he remembers the black and white tiles of the delicatessen floor more vividly than the smile of his mother or the touch of her hand. To punish himself for this treachery he will make himself remember the name of every kid in his kindergarten class—and there are those whose names he had never known, so he invents some, and there are others whose faces he can't summon up at all, empty places on bright red cushions. There was Ricky Hernandez, about whom his mother had made such a fuss, dazzling Ricky entirely that Nicky had been embarrassed throughout the entire event of his visit.

He hasn't invited anyone back since she died. This ordeal of homelife is something he has to experience alone.

It is the morning of his eleventh birthday. There is his empty cereal bowl, his glass for orange juice, his spoon—always the wrong one, his father puts out a soup spoon that Nicky doesn't have the heart to correct, so he will quietly replace it with a tea spoon, because that is how he likes to take his cereal, which spoon he will clandestinely clean and replace in the cutlery drawer, and put the unused soup spoon in the dishwasher. He doesn't believe in his power to hurt his father but he has promised his mother to be kind.

He hasn't heard his father leave but has grown tired of waiting, he is hungry and his bladder needs relieving and it is his birthday. He is eleven years old, coming closer into man's estate, there are changes he will be manifesting this year; for one, he will be leaving elementary school and starting junior high, a stage in life that he is considering changing his name for, and because it is his birthday, he has taken another step towards becoming the equal of his father. He assumes his place at the breakfast table with a kind of swagger.

His father does not wish him a happy birthday, which Nicky takes as a test, or a lesson in humility, or a game that his usually solemn father has decided that they should play this day. There will be cards later from his grandparents—his father's parents always mail theirs on the day itself, which means that Nicky won't receive it until the day after his birthday but that turns the event into a two-day festival, so he doesn't mind that, and there will be cards later when he gets back from school, from his aunt and from his mother's friends, who feel sorry for him, and apologetic too but he doesn't know what it is that they are apologising for, and there is the one that came yesterday from his mother's father who always sends it far too early, which means that the ones that do arrive in timely fashion come with their aura slightly spoiled, although that one always includes a ten-dollar bill, which buys his grandfather the right he supposes to send it as early as he cares to.

But this morning, the first of his twelfth year, his fingers graze the touch of perhaps bristle on his upper lip, he nods in companionable fashion to his father who is drinking an unscheduled second cup of coffee, and Nicky, who has not yet chosen the new name that will guide him through the next episodes of his life, is unmanned by the sight of his mother's handwriting on the envelope by his overlarge cereal spoon.

His father appears rapt in the act of reading the Times, the largest portion of the task seemingly being to unfold and refold it for a new column to become evident, which allows Nicky the privacy to touch the envelope with the fingers that have most recently been occupied in detecting possible forerunners of hair in multiple locations. There is no sign of the envelope having been tampered with. Risking a paper cut, he pushes his finger beneath the triangle flap on the back and can't quite cope with the gulp of realisation that it was his mother who had licked this envelope, which is more poignant even than her writing so boldly across it (and he wonders if, when he is thirteen maybe, or sixteen or twenty-one, he might achieve that confidence, and sincerity of purpose, to make his own writing so large), and it is his name and address on the front and the envelope has been stamped, which means that it had been too important to entrust to his father, and he is glad it hadn't been entrusted to his father, and he won't allow himself to wonder for quite some months, maybe even a year, when there won't be an equivalent envelope arriving on his twelfth birthday, about the mechanism by which this had been sent.

His father would have collected this with his correspondence when he got back from work the previous day, and he might not have looked at it until after his shower when he was sitting in the den, and maybe if they hadn't discontinued their practice of sitting uncomfortably together, his father might have as if casually tossed the card towards him, *I believe this one's for you, sport* . . . They hadn't eaten supper together because his father had gone out for something that he had troubled himself to tell Nicky about, a fundraiser for Beth Israel hospital, but all the same he would have known by then that this card had arrived, but he had kept it to himself, for its surprise to alarm his son.

He doesn't want to open it in front of his father, so he keeps stiffly to his routines of the morning, he pours himself a half-glass of orange juice and drinks it off, wiping his disappointingly unsullied mouth, and then pours himself a bowl of cereal and milk, doggedly getting through it with the wrong spoon while reading the back of the box, which informs him about grain production in Nebraska.

Planning his reply to his father's belated birthday wishes, he has settled on a brisk nod as the best response. He has toyed with the idea of a light chuckle followed by the question, *Oh is it? I'd forgotten* ... but he doesn't think he can carry that off quite as he might like. For one, his attempts at a light chuckle are not reliable, and on occasion produce a shrill giggle. For another, he does not trust his voice in conversation with his father, not on this day, with this envelope beside him. He fears the onset of tears.

Nicky waits out his father's departure. This is something that must be experienced alone. His father would have no end of self-important duties to perform. He only has school to go to. So Nicky, despite the clenching in his guts that this is costing him, pours himself a second bowl of cereal, and smiles indulgently upon his father's leave-taking. He hopes he hasn't displayed any unseemly triumph.

Before leaving, his father makes an unscheduled return to the kitchen.

'Happy birthday sport!' he says.

'Thank you,' Nicky says.

His father hands him another envelope, which contains a twenty-dollar bill and a brightly coloured birthday card that has a picture of a beach and a dog on it.

'I don't know if you want a party, you might be too old for that kind of thing, but maybe invite a few of the guys and have yourself a blast.'

Nicky doesn't know who in his father's mind might be 'the guys'. He is, socially speaking, on the edge of things.

'And maybe at the weekend, the two of us can celebrate? Take in a show.'

'Yes. Thanks Dad,' Nicky says.

Afterwards, he sits for some time on the toilet seat, but his system doesn't seem able to evacuate anything. Maybe it is a day for bringing in rather than pushing out. The day stretches invitingly ahead of him, as an occasion of sheer opportunity. He will save the moment of opening the card from his mother, and not out of dread but from choice. It will be the central point of his birthday, and it might be performed with ceremony—he knows where the candles are kept—or it might be done utterly casually.

He switches on the tv in his father's bedroom, and as he enjoys the cartoons, in a slightly removed sort of way, he wonders when it was that he had stopped designating this room as his *parents'* bedroom, and he castigates himself for this latest treachery. But then, making himself more comfortable by discarding the bolster, he considers whether he might be outgrowing cartoons. He isn't so primitive as to think that becoming eleven years old is the crossing of an actual threshold but all the same change is real so why mightn't it occur at ceremonial moments like this one?

After returning the bolster to its former position and sweeping out the shallow lines his body has impressed upon the comforter, he goes into his father's bathroom and inspects the items in the medicine cabinet. Taking a couple of sleeping pills, which might be useful in playground transactions, he goes into his own room and examines it critically. The posters from MAD magazine will have to go. The framed photograph of the day at the beach will be permitted to remain.

He lies, *ruminatively* he supposes, on his own bed. He wants now to open the card from his mother but he decides he should delay it further in case it turns out to be the end point to the day rather than its central one. His Charlie Brown backpack is inappropriate to his current mood and his new, permanently altered state. He borrows one of his father's attaché cases. Into it he puts the card from his mother and the lunch bag his father had prepared, customising it with the removal of the banana and the addition of two further peppermint patties. The attaché case still feels uncomfortably empty so he puts in one of his mother's books that he usually keeps on his shelf.

Jeans, converse, T-shirt, windbreaker, Mets cap, his father's briefcase, his birthday money, which, with his father's addition, amounts to thirty dollars, he is ready for his day. He rides the elevator down to the lobby practising his grip on the attaché case, which is more unwieldy than he had supposed. A two-handed grip is inappropriate. Inside it is what he now realises is a shoulder strap, which, graciously inclining his head to the invisible crowd making its rapturous applause, he works out how to buckle to the brass loops at either end of the top of the case.

With the strap slung over his left shoulder, the case bounces, a little awkwardly, against his right thigh, but he feels like an assassin with the parts of his rifle inside the briefcase. He probably has won awards for marksmanship and for his speed at assembling and disassembling his gun.

'How you doing Nicky.'

'Hi Tommy.'

'No school today? Hey it's your birthday isn't it. Happy birthday young man.'

He had been puzzling over his answer to the school question when the poignancy of the doorman having remembered his birthday hits him. So he deals with the questions with a shake of his head and a simultaneous, gruff *Thanks* and pulls the peak of his cap down in response to Tommy's salute.

It is a summer morning on Riverside Drive and many things are possible.

Nicky dawdles past the playground at Riverside Park, treating himself to some nostalgia and a first peppermint pattie. He has several destinations in mind, places he had been to with his mother. He might not make it out as far as Coney Island, but he will visit the Bronx Zoo and the 42nd Street Library and FAO Schwarz and the Automat and sit for a while in a meditative sort of way at the Frick. He thinks he might open his mother's card on the Staten Island Ferry.

At the newspaper booth on the corner of 116th Street he firmly shakes his head when Marquez tries to give him his customary copy of MAD. He asks for a copy of *Creem* instead, which he pays for and places inside his attaché case. He takes the 1 train down to Times Square.

Intending only the briefest of detours, he comes above ground to look at 42nd Street between Seventh Avenue and Broadway. This is not, in his parents' lexicon, a *safe* neighbourhood. He clenches his hands shut and open and shut trying to regather the sensation of his mother grabbing a tighter hold upon him to pull him towards safety.

A piece of her anxiety clings at him. He walks faster, edging through the people waiting to cross the road to put himself at their head. He shuts his eyes, he wants the grip of her hand holding tightly on to his, he is jostled forward, *Look alive kid!*, they are crossing the road and he is pushed along with them. Feeling like a puppet he exaggerates the movements of his arms and legs, jerking them erratically, and is gratified by the space this clears around himself.

He walks like that for a couple of blocks, jerking his limbs at random intervals. He tries muttering also but that feels like too much. At 39th Street he abates his movements, allows himself one lavish look behind, a contented sigh, as if his efforts have worked, as they always do for the master of disguise, this paid assassin. He rewards himself with a further peppermint pattie.

The master of disguise has missed Times Square entirely, and what he has heard described as the *fleshpots* of 42nd Street.

This has always created a very literal image for him, a carnival barker standing in front of a curtained doorway, with braziers at his side like the ones that the men on the Bowery gather around to warm themselves at in winter, except these would be metal baskets within which, writhing, are semi-autonomous heaps of flesh, muscle and breast and buttock and thigh and cheeks which still contain eyes that shriek in voiceless terror, because they have seen far too much, and these mounds of flesh would be lifting and falling, unable in their silent agony to do more than churn.

He walks along a cross street, unsure if he is going east or west. It is his birthday, his mother is still dead, but she is here with him also. He treads carefully, as she had taught him to do, alert for smouldering cigarette ends, discarded chewing gum, dog mess. His father's attache case slaps against his body with every second step. He waits to cross the next avenue, reflexively jerking his limbs in an absent-minded way to clear a space around himself.

Perhaps this would be the day when he takes up smoking. He might do many things.

He wants something new. When he goes to the Automat he will open a random hatch and eat something he has never tasted before. Or maybe he won't go to the Automat at all. That is a sentimentality that he should be training himself out of. He might eat anywhere. Try anything. A Chinese meal at the end of which he might be bold enough to ask for a second fortune cookie. He needs to keep back thirty-five cents for the subway ride back uptown. He has slightly more than that in change, and nearly thirty dollars left of birthday money, which gives him the budget to cover anything he wants, a Big Mac, a slice of pizza, a meal in an Italian restaurant, the sort of place that his mother called a *trattoria*. A French steak dinner. He won't be going toy shopping. He is putting that kind of thing behind him.

When people speak to him, he keeps his eyes down for street obstacles, walks faster. A ragged man on the corner of 39th and Sixth Avenue calls out to him, *Hey buddy, you got a smoke?* Which fills Nicky with an enormous pride that this man had called him buddy, and that he has been taken for a smoker. He begins the mime of a concerned patting of his pockets as if in pursuit of the cigarette pack that he had unaccountably neglected to carry but abandons the action as being a betrayal of their fellowship and demeaning to them both.

The Empire State Building is nearby. Twice at least, on days in the city with his mother, they had passed 34th Street and he had pleaded for them to go up to the observation deck. Uncharacteristically she had resisted this adventure, their complicity. Out of loyalty to her, he does not go there now. He heads north again, away from the spire, walking up Fifth Avenue. He stops to look into a jewellery shop window as if he is planning a heist.

Passing a playground, he wants very much to go on the slide and the swings. There are children there of about his own age, but they seem to be in the company of younger siblings, and he considers it beneath his dignity, even in solemnity, even in ceremony, even in memory, to enter, to play. He is someone who has been taken for a possessor of cigarettes, a comrade to gentlemen of the road, whose experience, of the heights of triumph, the depths of indignity, maybe even depravity, are beyond the common run of man. Someone like his father would not be included in this fellowship. The fact that he shares a name with his father, even in its diminutives, even in its mother-blessed inflections, is becoming monstrous to him. It had always been monstrous to him. That he should be Nicky, Little Nicky Sawyer, doomed to become Nick Sawyer and then Nicholas Sawyer, destined in his turn to sire another doomed child, Little Nicky Sawyer the Third, these are all shackles, the branding of a servitude to a man who has adopted a goatee, which, if his wife were still alive, if he had been sufficient of a man to keep his wife alive, he would never have been permitted to grow. Nicky will resist this doom. He hopes that on this day he might discover his actual name, his preferable, true name. His mother published books under the name of Hoffman. He too will be a Hoffman. The first name has not yet been revealed.

He moves on from the playground, glad to have detected something invitational in the eyes of a boy who has red hair and a reckless, capable manner, and glad too to have the strength of purpose to resist.

By the side of the 42nd Street Library he joins a small group of men observing a chess game. A white man of about his father's age in a business suit is playing a younger black man who is wearing a similar windbreaker to Nicky. The older man takes longer over his moves. After each one he taps the button on his side of the clock with a fastidious little click that is the most authoritative part of his game. Over the moves themselves, he struggles, reaching for a piece, then withdrawing his hand before allowing himself to commit to touching it. The younger man acts quickly, as if the making of decisions is incidental, happening outside of himself, as they wait for his inevitable victory to arrive, the other man's defeat, of which he is barely the mechanism. After each move he slaps down the button on his side of the clock, and waits, bored, for the next part of his opponent's agony to be over. The onlookers discuss possible moves despite the older man's obvious irritation, his scowl, *Guys, please!*, the way he tries to sit unmovably with his elbows at the board, his hands over his ears.

Nicky watches until the older man admits defeat. Or rather until he takes to repeatedly looking at his watch, as if it is time that is against him, *real* time, not chess time, as if other, more important moments crowd upon this one, so he can no longer give the best of himself to it . . . when even Nicky, whose knowledge of the game is rudimentary, can see that defeat has been upon him for the past few moves, had probably been upon him before they even sat down to play. The older man flicks over his king in a frustrated movement of capitulation to which the crowd assents with murmurs. The man beside Nicky says, *That's what I'm talking about!* The defeated player withdraws from his billfold a five-dollar bill, which he slides over to his victor, who accepts it with a slippery sort of motion and adds it to his own much larger roll and looks around for his next opponent, briefly resting his appraisal upon Nicky before moving on to someone more likely.

This is in the nature of a revelation. Nothing in Nicky's previous knowledge had led him to expect this kind of economic activity. The winner of the game is now playing another opponent, again it is a white man, but this one is much younger, a college student probably, an uptown Columbia type, to whom the champion allows a little more respect. He still radiates an aggressive boredom, he still slaps down his clock button at the conclusion of his moves, but he takes a little more time over them than he had for the previous game, paying this opponent the respect of examining the board with a larger part of his attention, and the courtesy of occasionally glancing at his face. Nicky stays beside the board until he is sure that the champion is going to win again, and then moves on.

He eats an ice cream sandwich in Central Park. This had been his mother's favourite. Formerly he had favoured brighter, icier things, popsicles and rainbow rockets, but he is becoming something new today.

At FAO Schwarz, he walks with solemn purpose—until he realises that this might be aping his father's customary pomposity, so he sloughs it off with a few spasmodic jerks of his arms and his legs, and lopes to the games department where he buys a chess clock. Annoyingly, it doesn't fit into his father's attache case so he has to carry an FAO Schwarz store bag which does not accord with the person he is becoming. He invents for himself a younger, more immature friend, perhaps named Raymond, who he used to play with when his mother was still alive. Raymond is ill, bed-bound, handicapped by a car accident maybe, or a stroke. Nicky is bringing something to his damaged friend, a present to lift his spirits in the sick room. He is carrying the bag as an act of mercy, a typical benevolence.

He still has most of his birthday money. Before leaving the store, he finds a toilet cubicle, where he slips his cash inside his sock because this is what he has heard is the correct thing to do with valuables when on the streets of the city.

A part of him, the weak part of him, or maybe the most romantic, wants to go back to the playground, find the red-haired boy, whose image has remained bright in his internal landscape. They might set off on the road together, move from town to town, he will earn a living by chess hustling, the red-haired boy would no doubt have an equivalent talent, maybe a supernatural balance and grace, a cat burglar, Nicky would play the marks at chess, keep their attention on the game, while the boy would spin through their mansions, almost with disdain slipping jewellery and stock certificates and the deeds to diamond mines into his bag. But this would make Nicky little more than a decoy, and any relationship should be an equal one. Also, much of the swag of millionaires would be kept behind the doors of safes. Which would require another in their gang, a safe-cracker, whom Nicky already mistrusts; he's called Frenchy and he has ice-cold blue eyes, and he's in the mansion with the red-haired boy, the two of them racing against the clock, the same pressures and urgencies upon them can only bring them closer together, and push away Nicky, who is doing barely more than playing a child's game. And they might need a getaway driver too, a scarred taciturn man with a past named Johnny. How could Nicky compete? He feels disgusted. They will need to find a better way of living their life.

Something troubling you my man?

The question is repeated.

'Me?' Nicky says, pointing, he realises fatuously, at himself.

'What's ailing you?'

'It's my birthday,' Nicky says, surprised that this is his immediate response.

'Hey! Happy birthday!'

'Thank you.'

The man talking to him is sprawled at the base of the low wall that separates the sidewalk of Central Park South from the Park itself. It is as if he has been dropped there and hasn't troubled to reorganise his body from the fall. He looks both utterly at ease and terribly uncomfortable.

'Take a load off.'

'Excuse me?'

'Sit down.'

The invitation is issued with an easy magnanimous charm

that Nicky decides he will devote as much time and trouble to emulate as might be necessary.

Nicky sits. He sits neatly, he hopes not too primly, with his back to the wall and his feet together and his knees pointing to the sky. He is, he discovers, glad to be sitting. He has done a lot of walking already in the course of his birthday.

'My name's Chambers.'

'I'm Nicky.'

Here had been an opportunity for a new name. He might have declared himself as Johnny or Frenchy or Chessmaster or anything and the moment for reinvention had taken him unawares and passed him by. He resolves to be more vigilant.

'Pleased to meet you Nicky. So. You got plans for the day? Your folks going to be throwing you a party?'

'I don't know.'

'Oh, a *surprise*. That's cool. We should better not talk about it. Keep the surprise.'

'My mother's dead.'

Chambers nods. He does Nicky the courtesy of not responding with an immediate expression of sympathy. Clearly he inhabits a world where mothers fall from tall buildings, and the people they leave behind know how to get on with their lives.

'She sent me a card.'

'How'd she do that?'

This is a good question, and Nicky appreciates that Chambers's curiosity had overcome his natural tact to ask it.

It is not a surprise to him that she has written. He ascribes to her, even in death, all kinds of magical powers. He hasn't even really questioned how the mechanics of this might have been arranged. He doesn't think you can go to the post office on the morning of your death and say, *Deliver this for me please in four years' time* . . . She might have given it to his father, but he doesn't believe that she would have given it to his father, and in that case there would have been no need for a stamp on the envelope. His father would have just said, in that awkward way he has, when he has something stored up that needs delivering, usually a reproach or a criticism, *By the way* . . .

'I don't know. She died just before I turned seven and I got a card from her for my birthday anyway. I guessed she'd given it to my aunt or someone to mail to me.'

'But you never found out.'

'No.'

'Maybe you didn't want to, is what I'm thinking. I don't know if I'd have wanted to in your situation. And you didn't get another one till now.'

'No.'

'And you haven't opened it yet.'

Nicky doesn't want to keep saying 'no' and Chambers doesn't need his suppositions to be confirmed just because they are correct, and Nicky doesn't want to encourage Chambers to ask the obvious next question, as to why he has delayed opening it. There would be a correct time to do so and he will recognise it when it arrives, and talking about any of this isn't necessary and he likes Chambers and doesn't want to rebuff him and he hopes that Chambers's tact will reassert itself.

'My mother's dead also,' Chambers says. 'She didn't think to write to me.'

This doesn't need a reply so Nicky doesn't offer one.

'How old are you today, birthday Nick?'

'Eleven.'

'And what you got in the bag?'

'Stuff. And I got a chess clock here.'

'You a grandmaster?'

'I'm not very good. I might be giving it to a friend in hospital.'

Again Chambers doesn't trouble them with an obvious response. They sit in a companionable silence. Chambers has very dark skin and is wearing an unseasonal dark green overcoat and black trousers and brown formal shoes without socks. The skin on his ankles is chafed a paler colour.

'How old are you, Chambers?'

'That's right,' Chambers says, which doesn't make a lot of sense in relation to the question, but Nicky assumes it corresponds to something internal.

People go past. A group of tourists climbs into a cart pulled by an aristocratic-looking horse, driven by a lady in a black waistcoat and top hat. The horse releases an enormous mound of excrement and then a second. Chambers doesn't seem to be bothered by the smell but it affects Nicky. Sitting for a while has alleviated the tiredness he'd raised by walking, and he is hit by two urgent things, the smell and the realisation that he is very hungry.

'I think I'm going to get something to eat,' he says.

'Where are you going to do that?'

'I don't know. Maybe the Automat. Or I'm guessing home. Uptown.'

Something prompts the next thing he says. He hopes it might have been his mother.

'Would you like to come? There'll be a lot of food in the house. I can make you lunch.'

'Might a shower also be available?'

This hadn't been in his thoughts. He'd imagined making them sandwiches from the refrigerator and then he'd work the coffee machine for Chambers and maybe walk him out to Riverside Park if he fancied being somewhere in nature.

'Yes, I'm sure,' he says.

'You might got to help me up here. My leg I think it died on me a little.'

They achieve it, working together. Chambers, who is taller than his prone position had led Nicky to expect, hops the circulation back into his legs.

'How we travelling?'

He squints at the road as if expecting a car to be available for them.

'We can walk over to Columbus Circle for the One Train. I live uptown.'

'Well let's get going.'

Chambers sets off at a fast pace that Nicky has to scamper to keep up with. At the station, Nicky puts in his token, Chambers, with an elegance and airborne sprawl of limbs, vaults over the turnstile beside him, and they are halfway down the stairs to the platform when Nicky realises they've left the FAO Schwarz bag behind.

'It's the universe telling you not to be a grandmaster,' Chambers says.

Nicky rides the 1 standing up, holding on to the pole as little as possible, feeling the carriage through the soles of his sneakers, swaying with its bumps and moves. Chambers slumps in his seat, which surprises Nicky because he has always assumed a code in which the squares sit down and the cool types, the gangsters and hipsters and deviants and delinquents, all stand.

They cross Broadway and walk up the long block of Riverside opposite the park.

'This a nice neighbourhood,' Chambers says, which isn't what his father says, or the members of his family, who live out of the city, in Long Island and Connecticut and New Jersey.

He hadn't considered the moment of their entry. There are times, particularly in cold weather, when there is no doorman out front. As well as their table inside the lobby, Tommy and Chrissy have a little room where they sort out the mail and drink coffee and smoke and fill out the *Daily News* crossword. But today is not cold weather. Maybe the universe, as Chambers might say, would ease them in, have their moment of arrival coincide with the doorman helping with the unloading of groceries from a car or an aged resident from a taxicab. It might be possible to sneak through to the elevator, ride up to the ninth floor unobserved. It isn't that he feels that they're doing anything wrong, but looking at them through others' eyes, he knows there is something incongruous about the sight of him and Chambers together.

There are no other residents in the lobby, and Tommy is there, sitting at the table, reading the paper. He stands up when he sees them enter the double doors, pulls down the peak of his cap as if something official is about to take place.

Chambers walks politely, but too meekly, which disappoints Nicky. He doesn't think Tommy is seeing the best of him.

Blocking Chambers's path, Tommy doesn't say anything, makes no joke with Nicky. He might be about to say, *Can I help you?* in an unmistakeable tone. He raises an eyebrow, expressing concern, maybe alarm, or as a friendly echo of the salute he would otherwise be making, and to warn Nicky of the inevitable call that is about to be made to Nicky's father at the hospital.

Both men are waiting for Nicky to take charge of the situation, which he does. Pulling out the remainder of his birthday money from his left sock, he hands it to Tommy. He has heard his father say, when Tommy or Chrissy have brought up some heavy objects from storage, *Get the kids something,* or, *Buy yourself a drink, on me.*

It doesn't come out quite right, because of the pressure of

the moment that is upon him, and he barely registers his own words, which he fears are something garbled like *Get the kids a drink . . . on me.* But the money has been passed over and he has twitched the sleeve of Chambers's overcoat and led him past Tommy and they are through the lobby and up the steps to the half-landing where the elevators are, and he presses the call button and the left-hand elevator opens its doors and the two of them are in and the doors are closing and Tommy is still standing there in the lobby, his hand opening and closing on the money.

Again, Nicky doesn't approve of the timidity that Chambers shows. He has to pull him into the apartment. He leads him past his own room and sits him in the living room which is where his parents had always received their guests.

'What can I offer you?' he says.

Chambers expands into the moment. 'Well, that is a question. I would enjoy a glass of scotch whisky, and a bite of food to accompany it, but first, I have to say, my wish would be to step into a shower if such a thing were available.'

'Of course. I'll get you a towel,' Nicky says.

This is not what he had been expecting, but he is happy to provide it and happy to demonstrate his mastery of his realm, to go into the linen cupboard, which still has the stickers on the shelves in his mother's writing, that designate the size of the towels and to which room the bedlinen belongs.

By the time Chambers has returned, wearing the white towelling robe that Nicky has provided from the master bedroom, Nicky has made peanut butter and jelly sandwiches. He is very hungry. He hopes he hasn't broken any rules of hospitality by devouring the first sandwich on his own.

'And a scotch?'

'If available. With ice. On the rocks, you might say.'

They sit at the dining table. Nicky has a glass of grape juice in a companion heavy tumbler to the whisky. They clink glasses and Chambers wishes him happy birthday, which makes Nicky feel like crying, but he is glad to be sharing this moment with his new friend.

'Do you play chess?'

'Sure. Sure I play chess. And if you're going to be fetching anything may I trouble you for a refresh of my glass?'

Nicky collects the bottle of whisky and the ice bucket and puts them on the table for Chambers to administer, hoping this satisfies the beverage part of his duties as host, and he retrieves the chess set from his father's den where it is kept on a low table, onyx figures that are light green and dark green, which means it is easy to get the two sides mixed up, which Chambers often does, sitting there swirling the scotch in his tumbler that he refreshes quite often, and piling in quantities of ice also; and Nicky lets his guest take back moves, even encourages him to do so when he foresees a move that will get his opponent into difficulty.

'I like making a sacrifice, Mister Nicky.'

In return he takes to calling Chambers, *Mister* Chambers, and the two of them reach a very pleasant state of congeniality.

It is interrupted by Mary from the hospital, who is a nurse and also works as a receptionist for his father's practice, who presents very sharp edges that the light shines off. He has never seen her in street clothes before.

She bustles into the living room as if engined. She waves her hands at Chambers, orders him out of *Doctor Sawyer's robe!* into his own clothes. Chambers goes into the bathroom and returns fully dressed, including his overcoat. He hands the bathrobe to Mary, who accepts it at arm's length and drops it on the floor.

'Your father is desperate with concern!' Mary says.

'What about?' Nicky says. He will put up a fight. This is his house, his guest, his birthday.

'Thank you Mister Nicky, I'd best be heading out now,' says Chambers, who leaves with his customary delicacy, but with a subservience that Nicky detests, that he blames himself for being in some way responsible for. Nicky has found two pairs of his father's socks, which he passes to Chambers as he is edging out of the door.

'Your father will be home soon,' Mary says, as if this is the end point to all meaning.

Nicky retreats into his bedroom. He intends to remain there, perhaps for ever.

Inside the envelope is a card and inside the card, folded twice, so it is a third of its size, is a pale blue sheet of paper.

On the front of the card is a reproduction of one of those

paintings that his mother likes so much of a foreign interior that always have such a heaviness about them that they make him sleepy.

He looks up at the ceiling as if somehow she might be watching him from above. Three strings dangle from the ceiling from which used to be suspended model planes that he has cut down because he is putting away childish things.

He doesn't unfold the letter straight away because he doesn't want it to be a disappointment. But of course it won't be a disappointment. Everything, even the sentimentality, is written in her voice, in the knowledge of the complicities that they share, which barely need referring to.

The sheet of paper on which the letter is written is so thin that to read the words he rests the page against the back of the envelope because otherwise the writing on one side of the page is encroached upon by the back-to-front writing of the other. He reads it quickly and there is no need yet to concentrate on its meaning or implications, just enjoy the swirl of her handwriting, the generous loops her pen makes, the huge mass of feeling that it exposes, that channels that flow between them.

He folds it up again and returns it to the envelope and places it in front of himself on the bed, upon which he sits cross-legged, and everything might be messy and out of place around them but the letter is perfectly centred on the bed, its edges parallel with the sides. And then he opens it again, and reads it through, and then he reads it through again, but slowly, enjoying each sentence in the knowledge of the next sentence to come, as if it is a poem that already lives in his memory. And then he folds it again and puts it in its envelope again because he is anxious that there is an energy to this letter that he mustn't be careless with, allow it to dissipate so that there might come a time when he will need to call upon it and there will be nothing to call upon, just navy-blue words written in a big scrawl on sky-blue correspondence paper.

The energy will not discharge itself. Although he does remain prudent with it. He will not ever show it to anyone else, no matter how curious others might be, like his father, with his effortful *Hey buddy* when Nicky eventually comes out of his room that evening.

Mary is still in the apartment. Nicky consents to eat some of the takeaway they'd ordered. He manages a spring roll and some sweet and sour pork so he might be permitted a fortune cookie.

'We'll talk in the morning,' his father says. Nicky says nothing because there is nothing to say.

His father will want to know how he was referred to in the letter, what accusations have been made against him, and his father had never truly known Nicky's mother if he thinks she might corrupt this moment with accusations.

Opening it again, the returning sight of her writing does bring up the tears that have been threatening to emerge all day.

He reads it even more slowly this time, hearing her voice in each word. He promises her that he will become astonishing, that he will be kind. He doubts the prophecy of her penultimate line that one day he will forgive his father.

This book has been typeset by
SALT PUBLISHING LIMITED
using Neacademia, a font designed by Sergei Egorov for the
Rosetta Type Foundry in Czechia. It has been manufactured
using Holmen Book Cream 65gsm paper, and printed and
bound by Clays Limited in Bungay, Suffolk, Great Britain.

CROMER
GREAT BRITAIN
MMXXVI